wonderful time between magic and so-called rationality."

g, co-creator of the Logo programming language, on the early days of Logo

First Second
s an imprint of Roaring Brook Press,
Holtzbrinck Publishing Holdings Limited Partnership
nue, New York, New York 10010

n-Publication Data is on file at the Library of Congress

SBN: 978-1-62672-076-3
SBN: 978-1-62672-340-5

may be purchased in bulk for promotional, educational,
use. Please contact your local bookseller or the Macmillan
and Premium Sales Department at (800) 221-7945 x5442
at MacmillanSpecialMarkets@macmillan.com.

on 2016

gn by Rob Steen

China by Toppan Leefung Printing Ltd., Dongguan City, Guangdong Province

k: 10 9 8 7 6 5 4 3 2 1
er: 10 9 8 7 6 5 4 3 2 1

GENE LUEN YANG
& MIKE HO

New York

"It was this

–Wally Feurze

New York

Published by
First Second i
a division of
175 Fifth Av

Cataloging-i

Paperback I
Hardcover

Our books
or business
Corporate
or by emai

First editi

Book des

Printed i

Paperba
Hardco

Chapter

So were you able to write that program?
What?!
I don't know how to What.
I have no idea what's going on, and I might get kicked out of school?! This is bunk!
Josh! No stupid questions, remember? Eni and I got this!
I hoped we had it, anyway. Let me tell you what we did.
Just listen and learn.
This Path Portal is just a hexagon with lines sticking out of it, right?
Right. So let's start with OpenSesame, the program that makes the turtle walk a hexagon.
I'm gonna write it out with my chalk. It'll help us think.

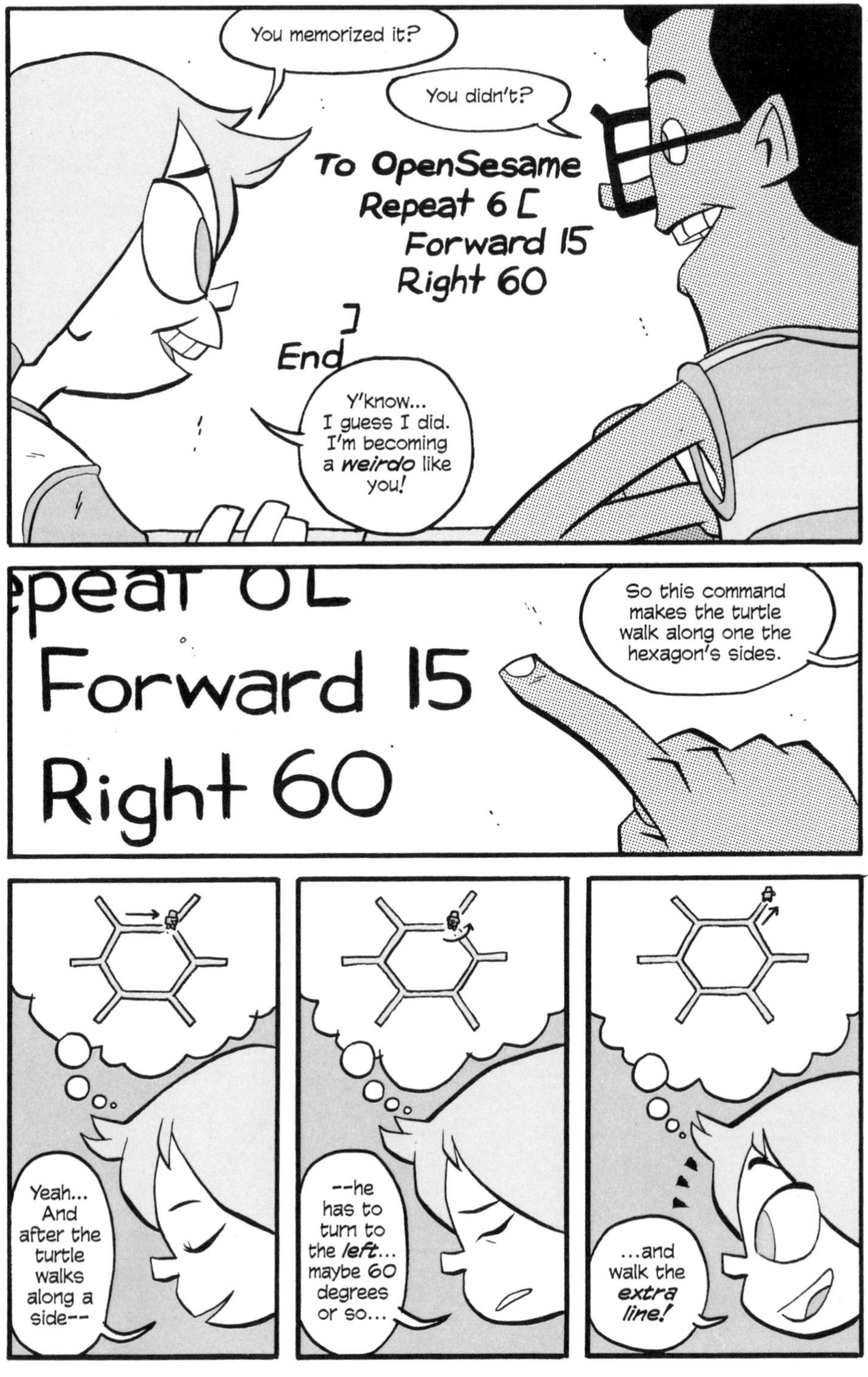
You memorized it?
You didn't?
To OpenSesame
Repeat 6 [
Forward 15
Right 60
]
End
Y'know... I guess I did. I'm becoming a *weirdo* like you!
Forward 15
Right 60
So this command makes the turtle walk along one the hexagon's sides.
Yeah... And after the turtle walks along a side--
--he has to turn to the *left*... maybe 60 degrees or so...
...and walk the *extra line!*

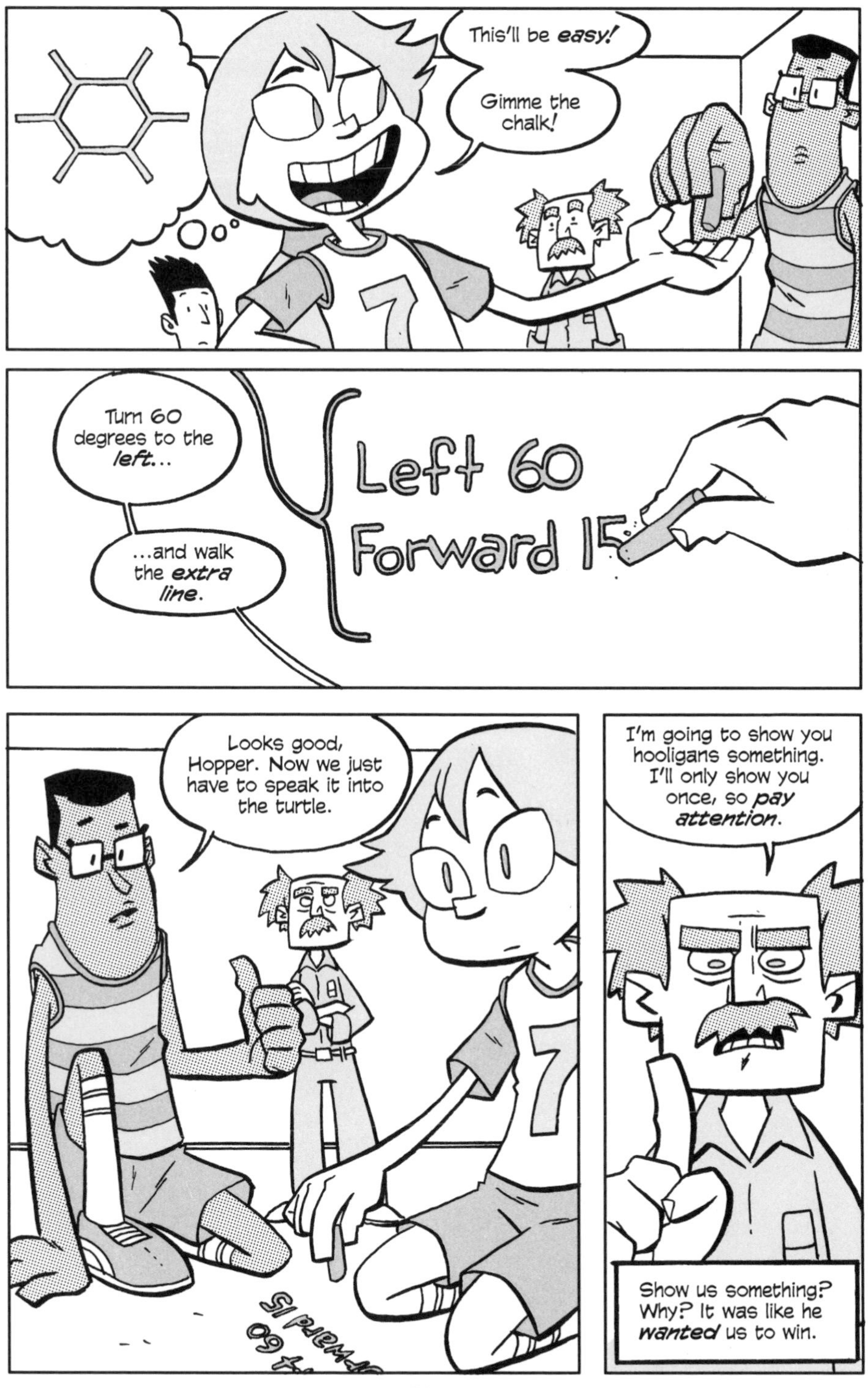
This'll be *easy!*
Gimme the chalk!
Turn 60 degrees to the *left*...
...and walk the *extra line*.
Left 60
Forward 15
Looks good, Hopper. Now we just have to speak it into the turtle.
I'm going to show you hooligans something. I'll only show you once, so *pay attention*.
Show us something? Why? It was like he *wanted* us to win.

?
EdAll
Whoa! You're even cooler than I thought, Little Guy!
Neat.
EdAll is short for "Edit All."
You can edit all the turtle's programs using this keyboard and screen.
Back 10
Right 60
Back 30
Right 60
]
End
You can also type in what you've written on the ground as a new program, but you'll have to give it another name.
The turtle already knows a program called OpenSesame.
No problem!
erase erase
GRACIE-

How about this for a name?
Um...
WRITE WRITE
All right, here we go...
Where's the T key? T... T...
There!
TK
Now where's the O? O... O...
Oh, for crying out loud! We'll all be skeletons by the time you're done! Move!
!
You're looking at the fastest typist at Stately Academy!
It's true. He's got trophies at home.
Stately Academy gives trophies for typing? That's stupid.

To HopperRocks
Repeat 6 [
Forward 15
Left 60
Forward 15
Right 60
]
End
Done!
My typing's even more *wicked* than my sky hook!
SHUT
Whatever. About time you made yourself *useful*, Josh.
All right, then. Moment of truth.
?
HopperRocks
Why, Eni! How sweet of you to finally admit it!

What--?!
Unfortunately for me, Little Guy proved that I definitely did *not* rock.
What the heck was *that?*
That was a poorly coded program.

You *failed*, children! Tomorrow, I will request a meeting with Principal Dean.
My parents are gonna kick me out of the house!
Mr. Bee, one more chance, please! We can fix this!
You knew the risks when you accepted my challenge!
Hopper, come here.
I'll have to live in a cardboard box!
Young lady--!
Excuse me!
This is where we went *wrong*. We need *more instructions* here, after the turtle walks the extra line.
To HopperRocks
Repeat 6[
Forward 15
Right 60
]
End
Left 60
Forward
Yeah, I see it! After he walks the extra line, he has to *come back* to continue walking the hexagon!
He needs to *turn* all the way around--
--*go back* to the hexagon--

--and turn *left*, to get ready to walk the next side!
An agreement is an agreement!
Shhh. We're coding.
We just need three more instructions to tell the turtle to--
ERASE
ERASE
Forward 15
Right 180
Forward 15
Left 60
--turn all the way around--
--walk back--
--and turn left!
Hey, Josh--
Already on it!
TK
TK
TK

How does that look?
To JoshRules
Repeat 6 [
Forward 15
Left 60
Forward 15
Right 180
Forward 15
Left 60
]
End
Good, except you gave the program a stupid name.
I don't see anything wrong with it.
You mean, besides that it's the *biggest lie in the world?!*
Guys, quit bickering. Let's give it a try.
?
JoshRules
We all held our breath.
Even *Mr. Bee,* which confirmed it for me. Deep down, he was actually rooting *for* us.

All right now, Little Guy. You're gonna repeat the commands between the brackets *six times*...
To JoshRules
Repeat 6 [
Forward 15
Left 60
Forward 15
Right 180
Forward 15
Left 60
]
End
To JoshRules
Repeat 6 [
Forward 15
Left 60
Forward 15
Right 180
Forward 15
Left 60
]
End
To JoshRules
Repeat 6 [
Forward 15
Left 60
Forward 15
Right 180
Forward 15
Left 60
]
End

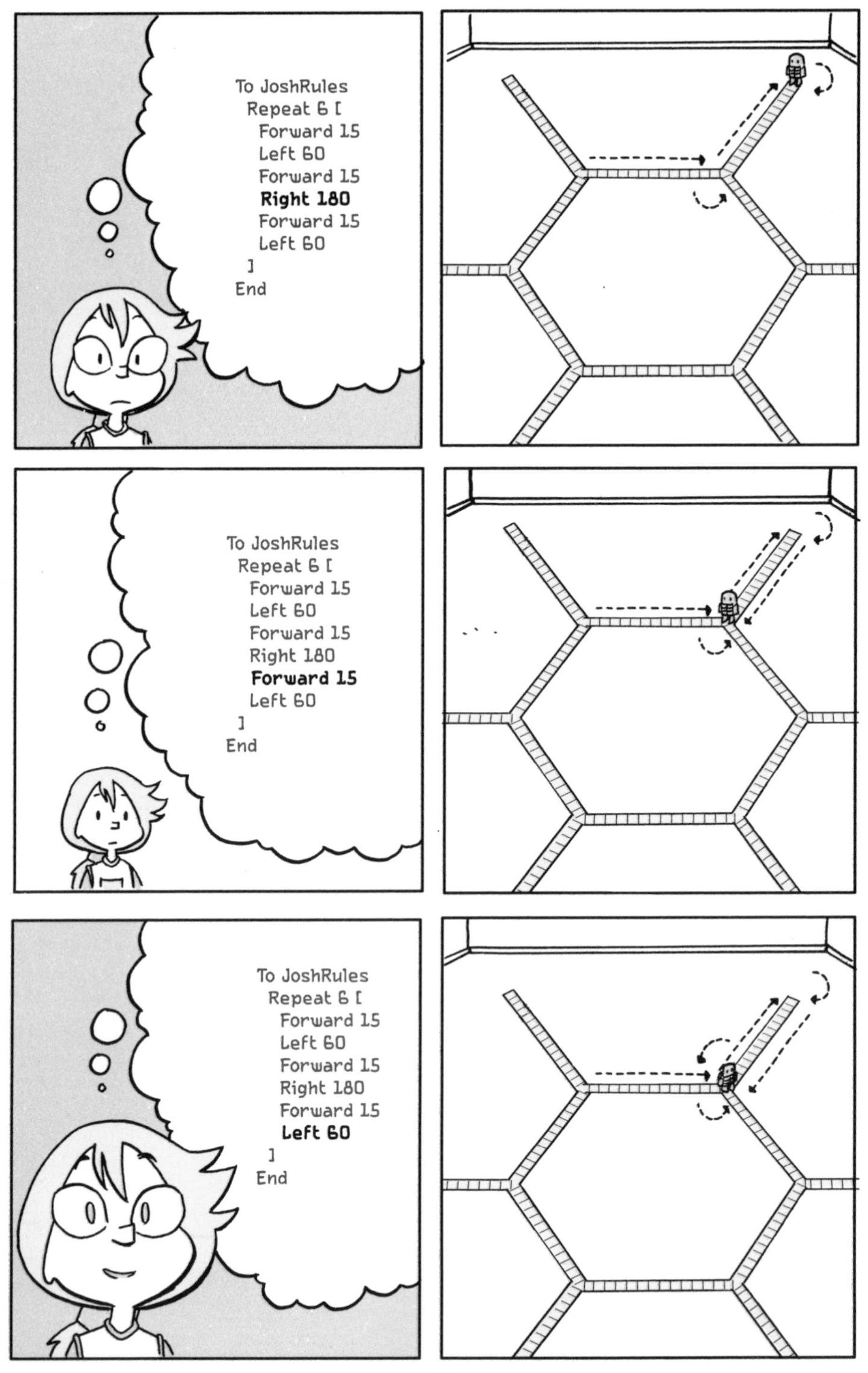
To JoshRules
Repeat 6 [
Forward 15
Left 60
Forward 15
Right 180
Forward 15
Left 60
]
End
To JoshRules
Repeat 6 [
Forward 15
Left 60
Forward 15
Right 180
Forward 15
Left 60
]
End
To JoshRules
Repeat 6 [
Forward 15
Left 60
Forward 15
Right 180
Forward 15
Left 60
]
End

One down, five to go! Now for the second repetition...
To JoshRules
Repeat 6 [
Forward 15
Left 60
Forward 15
Right 180
Forward 15
Left 60
]
End
Once the turtle began on the second side of the hexagon, I knew.
We did it. We'd traced the Path Portal *perfectly*.

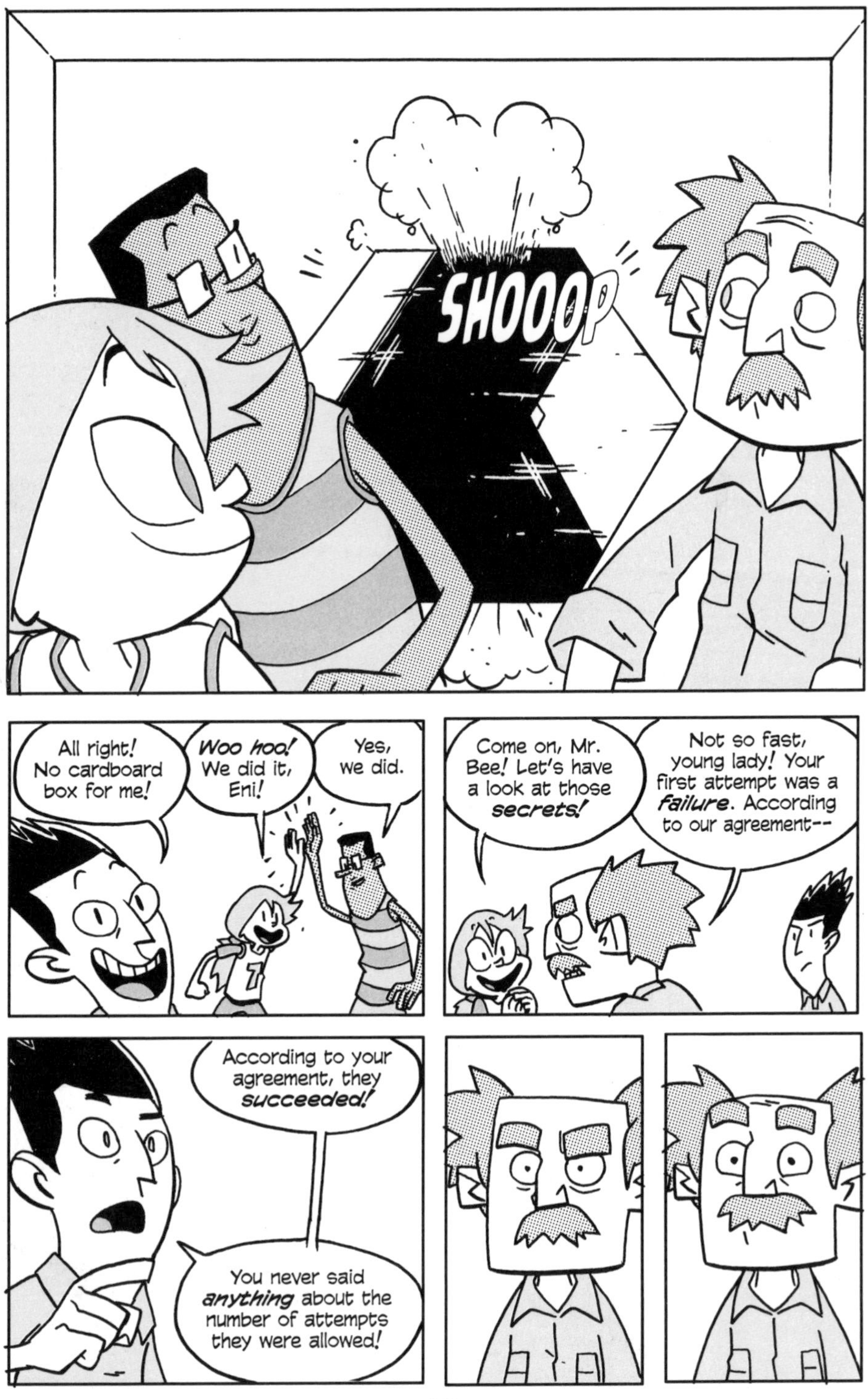
SHOOOP
All right! No cardboard box for me!
Woo hoo! We did it, Eni!
Yes, we did.
Come on, Mr. Bee! Let's have a look at those secrets!
Not so fast, young lady! Your first attempt was a failure. According to our agreement--
According to your agreement, they succeeded!
You never said anything about the number of attempts they were allowed!

Very well. Follow me.
Quick thinking, Josh.
Yeah. Not bad.
Admit it. Josh rules!
Eh. I wouldn't go that far.
Children, you must promise to keep secret what I'm about to reveal to you!
We promise, Mr. Bee.
Stately Academy is built on the grounds of another learning institution, long abandoned, called the Bee School.
Bee...like your last name?
Many years ago, I myself founded the Bee School. Though most of the old campus has been demolished, a few underground classrooms still exist...

...like this one.
Whoa!
Check out all these *robot turtles!*
Do they all speak the same language as this turtle?
Yes, a language called *Logo*.
By the standards of the computer world, it is *ancient* and all but *lost*.

Mr. Bee, what's this over here?

LOGO PRIMITIVE COMMANDS
Forward
Back
Right
Left
PenUp
PenDown
PenPaint
PenErase
SetPenColor
Random
Print
Label
Make
To
End
Repeat
While
If
IfElse
It's exactly what it says it is-- a list of Logo's *primitive commands*.
These are the commands every turtle knows as soon as it's *created*, before it learns any new commands.

Turtles can learn commands?
Of course. When you write programs, you teach the turtle *new commands*.
This one knows not only *Forward* and *Right* and *Left*--
--but also the commands we taught it, like *OpenSesame* and *JoshRules*.
That's right.
Woohoo! *Josh rules!*
So Mr. Bee... you were once a teacher?
A teacher, a professor, a mentor...and perhaps, if I may be so bold, a *visionary!*

At the Bee School, everyone learned and everyone taught.
The *faculty* learned by teaching the *students* how to interact with our robots.
And the *students* learned by teaching the *robots* new commands.
Our robots weren't meant to be mere *appliances*. They were meant to be *instruments of art!*
REMOVE!
They weren't meant to hold *leaf blowers*. They were meant to hold *pens*.
SNAP!
Hm. So that's what the commands PU and PD mean.
Good deduction, lad! *PU* and *PD* are shortened versions of *PenUp* and *PenDown*.
Take a look at this. A piece of *art*, created by one of my students many years ago.

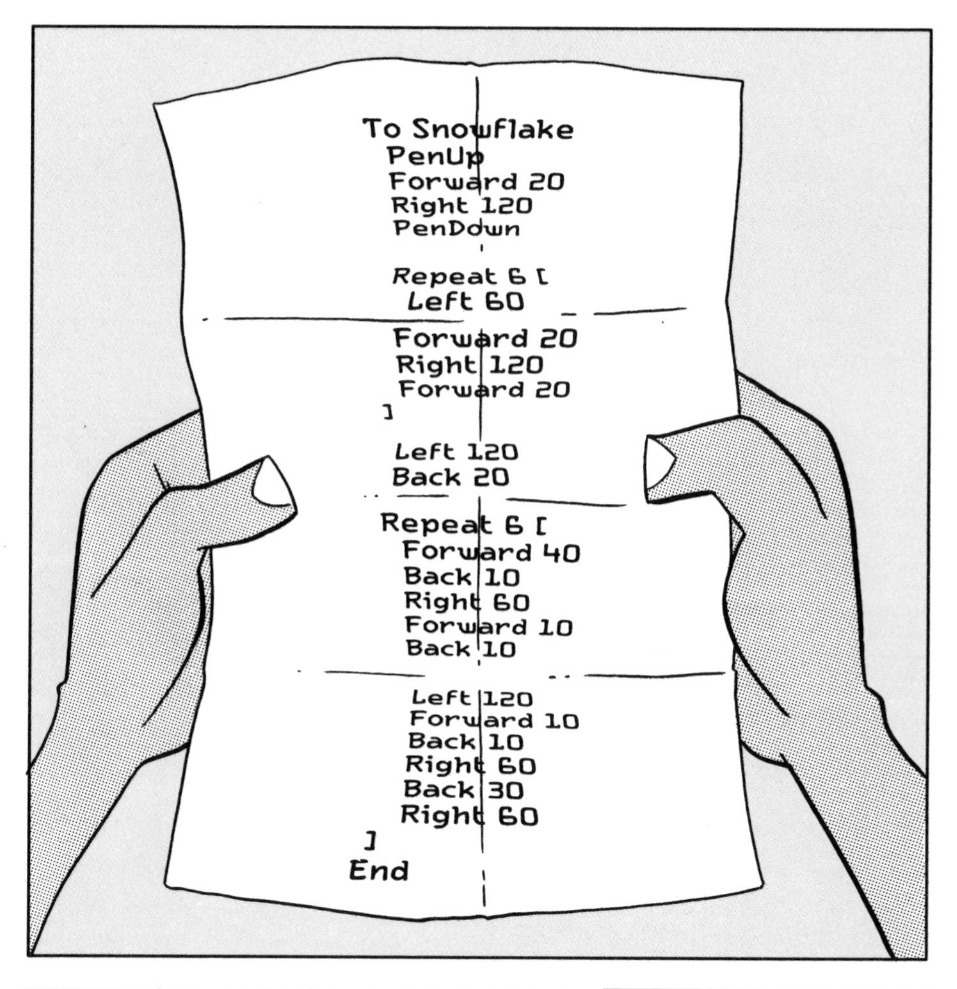
To Snowflake
PenUp
Forward 20
Right 120
PenDown
Repeat 6 [
Left 60
Forward 20
Right 120
Forward 20
]
Left 120
Back 20
Repeat 6 [
Forward 40
Back 10
Right 60
Forward 10
Back 10
Left 120
Forward 10
Back 10
Right 60
Back 30
Right 60
]
End

It's already keyed into this turtle. Go on. Give it a try.

?
Snowflake

Wicked!

The Bee School sounds amazing!
Way better than Stately Academy!
More than amazing. It sounds like a utopia.
Oh, in many ways it was. A utopia built upon my deepest ideals about human nature and technology.
But why would you shut a place like that down, Mr.-- uh, I mean, Professor Bee?
Yeah, and become a janitor?
...
Because I was wrong.
About both human nature and technology.

When I got home that night, I tiptoed into my room as quietly as I could.
It was no use. Mom was already there.
!
Where have you been?
CLICK!
Basketball practice ran late.
It's ten o'clock!
We take the sport very seriously!
Have you finished all your homework?
Oh...uh... of course!
Don't lie, Hopper. You haven't even touched your Mandarin worksheet!
You went through my backpack?! That's an invasion of privacy!

I don't need you constantly breathing down my neck, Mom! I'm old enough to mind my own business!
If that were true, your Mandarin homework would be done!
It's not due until third period anyway! That gives me the whole morning to finish it!
For you, this assignment is due in one hour.
What?! You're abusing your motherly powers! You can't just change due dates for one student!
I just did.
If Dad were here, he'd never let you do this to me!
...
Slip the worksheet beneath my door in an hour or it will be marked late.

Aaargh! Just so you know, your homework is the ***stupidest*** homework in the ***entire school!***
Repeating the same strokes over and over--it's not for humans, it's for ***robots!***
Robots.
So I borrowed without asking.
I didn't think Professor Bee would mind.
After all, Eni had done it and he didn't get in all that much trouble.
Not counting the parts where we were attacked by ***binary birds*** and then almost got ***expelled***, of course.
?
PenDown
PLINK!
This turtle was smaller than the one Eni and I found in the janitor's closet. ***Way*** smaller--about the size of an eraser.

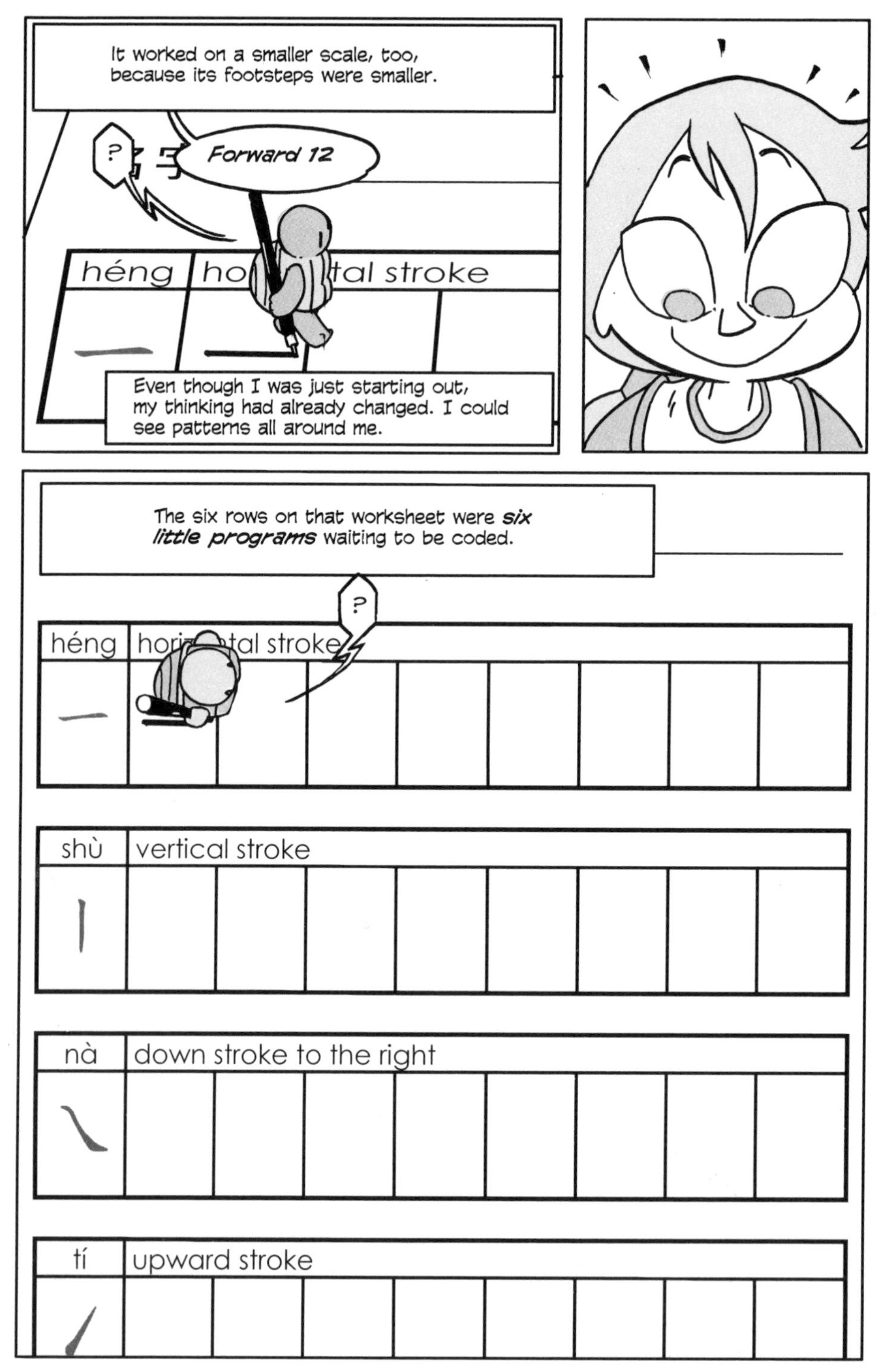
It worked on a smaller scale, too, because its footsteps were smaller.
?
Forward 12
héng
Even though I was just starting out, my thinking had already changed. I could see patterns all around me.
The six rows on that worksheet were *six little programs* waiting to be coded.
?
héng
shù
vertical stroke
nà
down stroke to the right
tí
upward stroke

I closed my eyes and did the first one.
Repeat 7 [
PenUp
Forward 4
PenDown
Forward 12
]

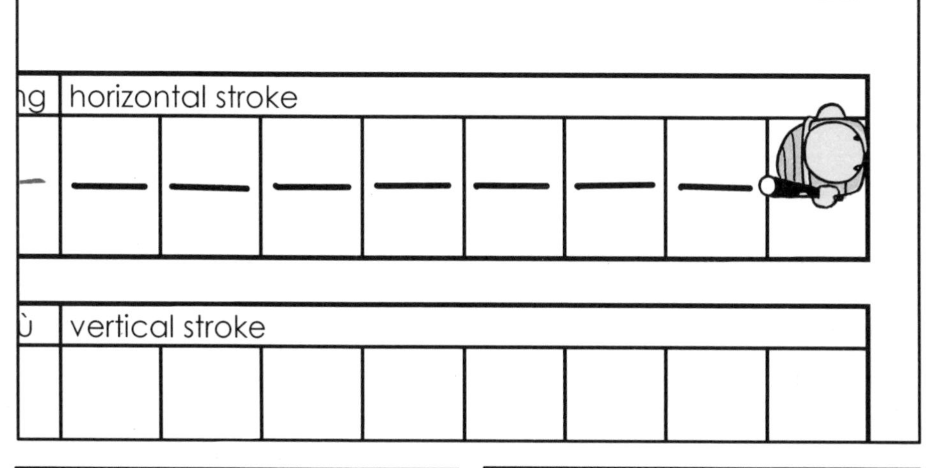
horizontal stroke
vertical stroke

Worked like a charm.
Yes!

名字: ___________________

héng	Okay, I'm gonna pause for a moment and give you a chance to think.
shù	cal stroke
nà	down stroke to the right
tí	upward stroke
diǎn	dot
pié	down stro

Try to figure out how I did that next row on the worksheet.

It's a series of ***eight*** up-and-down lines. Each one is ***twelve*** steps long, and they're ***sixteen*** steps apart from one another.

The turtle starts at the top of the first line, facing ***right***.

Go ahead, give it a shot. Try to write a program that can do my homework.

Chapter

Compared to Professor Bee's Path Portals, the Mandarin worksheet wasn't all that bad.
shù
vertical stroke
Turn right--
--draw a line--
--and then get in position to draw the next line.
Repeat that *eight* times and we're done!
?
There are lots of different ways to draw those 8 lines. Here's how I did it:
Repeat 8 [
Right 90
PenDown
Forward 12
PenUp
Left 90
Forward 16
Left 90
Forward 12
Right 90
]

Perfect!
shù vertical stroke
down stroke to the
Does your program look similar? There's no one right answer here. Yours can look *different*, but still be right.
It took me almost an hour to figure out the rest of the rows.
?
Repeat 8 [
Right 45
PenDown
Forward 12
PenUp
Back 12
Left 45
Forward 16
]
I gotta admit, I probably could've finished the worksheet myself in about ten minutes.
?
Repeat 8 [
Right 135
PenDown
Forward 10
PenUp
Back 10
Left 135
Forward 16
]

But getting the turtle to do it was just so much more *satisfying*.
?
Repeat 8 [
Right 45
PenDown
Forward 6
PenUp
Back 6
Left 45
Forward 16
]

After all, *robotic tasks* ought to be done by *robots*.
?
Repeat 8 [
Right 90
PenDown
Forward 8
Right 25
Forward 4
Right 25
Forward 4
PenUp
Back 4
Left 25
Back 4
Left 25
Back 8
Left 90
Forward 16
]

名字:
héng horizontal stroke
shù vertical stroke
nà down stroke to the right
tí upward stroke
diǎn dot
piě down stroke to the left
We make a pretty good team, don't we, Little...er, *Mini* Guy?
I thought it turned out pretty well.

Mom disagreed, of course.
The next morning, she dropped me off at Principal Dean's office as soon as we got to school.
Ms. Hu believes you cheated, Hopper.
Hey, you know my name this time. *Gold star*, Principal Dean.
She's right, of course. These sorts of worksheets must be done *by hand*. You clearly used a *machine* of some sort. I suppose I ought to punish you--
--but to be honest, I'm *impressed!* This is remarkable work!
!
Y-you really think so?
Calibrating a machine to perform such *precise* work is no small feat, Hopper! Tell me, what sort of machine was this? A small robot, perhaps?
Would you be willing to give me a demonstration?
I wanted to show him the robot *so badly*, to convince him that the students of his school shouldn't be subjugated to such pointless *busy work*.
And even more than that, I wanted to brag to an adult--*any adult*--about all the programs I'd created.

But something about his smile made me not trust him.
Nope. No robot here.
Guess I've just got a *steady hand*.
...
Three more weeks of *trash duty* and no credit for this assignment.
You are *excused*.
Fine.
One more thing. Ms. Hu isn't just your *teacher*, is she? She's also your *mother*.
Yeah. So?
Hm.
The *rugby team* should be waiting outside my office. Show them in, then get to class.

You guys the rugby team? Principal Dean's ready for you.
Sniff! Sniff! Hey, fellas, you smell that?
Yeah... smells like dork.
You mean, basketball player?
Whatever. Same thing.
Har har har!
Oh, grow up!
Sorry to break it to you, Dork Girl, but if there's no tackling, it's not a real sport!

What're you kids doing here? I've already told you my secret! Now leave me to my work!
Principal Dean told us to report to you for three weeks of trash duty.
Six for me.
Really? Why?
I don't wanna talk about it.
So how about we get started, Professor?
When we are in public, you will address me as Mr. Bee.
Eni! Hopper! Wait up!

Go away, Josh! Being nice for a couple hours yesterday does not make up for several days' worth of *jerk-face behavior!*
Aw, come on!
Why aren't you hanging out with Joshie?
Mr. Bee, I want *trash duty!*
Ludicrous! You haven't done anything wrong!
WHAP
OW!
How about now?
Very well.
Two hooligans or *three*, it makes little difference to me.
Come along.

Whoa. How many underground classrooms are there?
A few. There used to be many more.
The turtles here are in charge of various tasks around campus: mowing the lawn, cleaning the whiteboards, sweeping up the trash.
Here, take these. I'm sure you'll do a slower, sloppier job than my turtles, but what can I do? Principal Dean wants you punished.
Hopper, check this out.
Another program?
To SquareLawn
Make "Length 1
Repeat 40 [
Forward :Length
Make "Length (:Length + 1)
Right 90
]
End
Yeah. I think it makes something beautiful.
Looks like gobbledygook to me.

Of course it looks like gobbledygook to you. You're a *dummy*.
That's a program I wrote for my *lawn-mowing turtle*.
What's this instruction do, Professor Bee?
It sets up a *variable* called *Length*, with a value of *one*.
To SquareLawn
Make "Length 1
R eat 40 [
orward :Length
Make "Length (:Le
Right 90
Okay, now *that* was gobbledygook.
A variable is...think of it as a *little box* inside the turtle's brain. The turtle uses it to store *numbers* and other sorts of data.
Okay, let me think this through. When he follows that instruction, the turtle will make a *box* inside his brain--
--name it *"Length"*--
LENGTH
--and put a *one* inside.
LENGTH
1

But why? Who would want a little box inside their brain?
How about this line here?
To SquareLawn
Make "Length 1
Repeat 40 [
Forward :Length
Make "Length (:Length + 1)
Right 9
]
End
That tells the turtle to add one to the value inside Length. Think of it in three steps:
The turtle takes the number stored in Length--
Make "Length (:Length + 1)
LENGTH
1
--adds one to it--
Make "Length (:Length + 1)
1+1=2
--and puts the resulting number back into Length.
Make "Length (:Length + 1)
LENGTH
2
So Length changes from one to two.
It will the first time. But notice these instructions are in a Repeat command, so the turtle will do them over and over.

I still don't get it.
I think I kinda get it--
--because, y'know, I'm not a *dummy*--
--but I'd get it even better if I could see it in *action!* Let's try running the program! The lawn-mowing turtle is this big guy, right?
No, no!
He works on *too large* a scale! If you activate him in here, he'll *wreck* this entire room!
Let's type the program into *Little Guy* and tell him to run it.
Wait. You've got him with you all the time now, wherever you go?
That's not *normal*, Eni. Not normal at all.
Put a *PenDown* command at the very top so we can see the path he's walking.
All done!
To JoshHasBigBiceps
PenDown
Make "Length 1
Repeat 40 [
Forward :Length
Make "Length (:Length + 1)
Right 90
]
End
You just *had* to change the program's name to something stupid, didn't you?
If by "stupid" you mean *true*, then *yes*.

?
JoshHasBigBiceps
To keep myself from decking Josh, I focused on what the turtle was doing.
To JoshHasBigBiceps
PenDown
Make "Length 1
Repeat 40 [
Forward :Length
Make "Length (:Length + 1)
Right 90
]
End
LENGTH
1
All right, Little Guy, you're gonna repeat the next three lines *forty* times!
To JoshHasBigBiceps
PenDown
Make "Length 1
Repeat 40 [
Forward :Length
Make "Length (:Length + 1)
Right 90
]
End
LENGTH
1
1
To JoshHasBigBiceps
PenDown
Make "Length 1
Repeat 40 [
Forward :Length
Make "Length (:Length + 1)
Right 90
]
End
LENGTH
2

To JoshHasBigBiceps
PenDown
Make "Length 1
Repeat 40 [
Forward :Length
Make "Length (:Length + 1)
Right 90
]
End
LENGTH
2
One down, thirty-nine to go!
To JoshHasBigBiceps
PenDown
Make "Length 1
Repeat 40 [
Forward :Length
Make "Length (:Length + 1)
Right 90
]
End
LENGTH
2
2
To JoshHasBigBiceps
PenDown
Make "Length 1
Repeat 40 [
Forward :Length
Make "Length (:Length + 1)
Right 90
]
End
LENGTH
3
To JoshHasBigBiceps
PenDown
Make "Length 1
Repeat 40 [
Forward :Length
Make "Length (:Length + 1)
Right 90
]
End
LENGTH
3

Two down, thirty-eight to go!
To JoshHasBigBiceps
PenDown
Make "Length 1
Repeat 40 [
Forward :Length
Make "Length (:Length + 1)
Right 90
]
End
3
LENGTH
3
To JoshHasBigBiceps
PenDown
Make "Length 1
Repeat 40 [
Forward :Length
Make "Length (:Length + 1)
Right 90
]
End
3
LENGTH
4
To JoshHasBigBiceps
PenDown
Make "Length 1
Repeat 40 [
Forward :Length
Make "Length (:Length + 1)
Right 90
]
End
LENGTH
4
Eni was right.

After *forty* repetitions, the program made something ***beautiful***.
That's even cooler than the snowflake!
"Cooler than the snowflake!" ***Ha ha!*** Get it?
You're touching me.

Professor, I've been meaning to ask you...
How'd you know my dad's name?
BRIIIING
Lunch is over. Off to class with you.
But-but-
But we never did our *trash duty*. Aren't you going to get in trouble, Professor Bee?
Aren't *we* gonna get in trouble?
Not to worry. I'll have turtles take care of it after school.
I *prefer* it that way, truthfully. *Robots* are much better at those sorts of precise, repetitive tasks.
You are *students*. Go *learn*.
SHUF
You really need to talk to my mom, Professor!

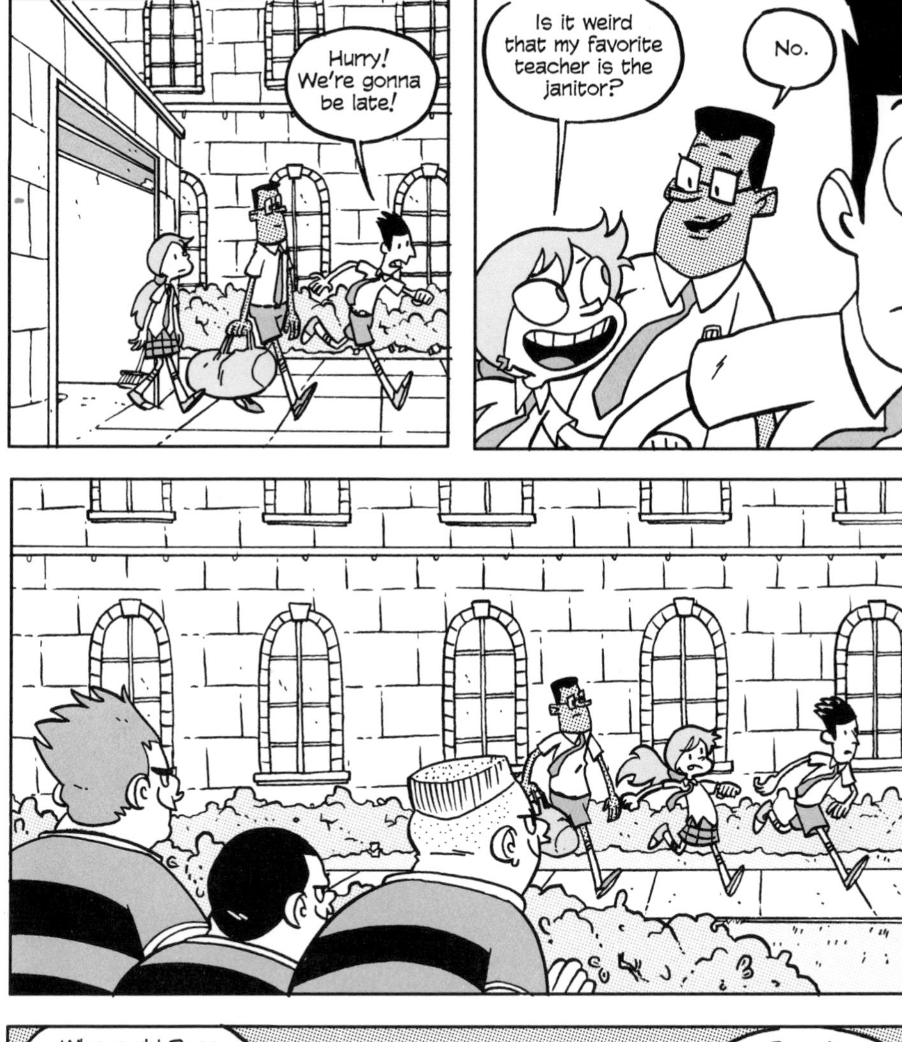
Hurry! We're gonna be late!
Is it weird that my favorite teacher is the janitor?
No.

Why would Dean care what that *Dork Girl* and her little dork buddies are up to?
Does it matter? You want new uniforms or not?

How was school?
Started off the day with a visit to the principal's office. Spent all of lunch on trash duty.
"Trash duty" ought to be in quotes, really, and it was the *highlight* of my whole day. But Mom didn't need to know that.
You know, typical day for a *delinquent kid* from a *broken home*.
Hopper, stop it!
And sit down. We need to talk.
I'm not sure how you did your worksheet. Did you use the computer?
...
It doesn't matter. I need you to take your Mandarin homework more *seriously*. You have to do it *by hand*.
Your assignments are stupid! I'm not a *robot*, Mom!
Let me show you something. Please.

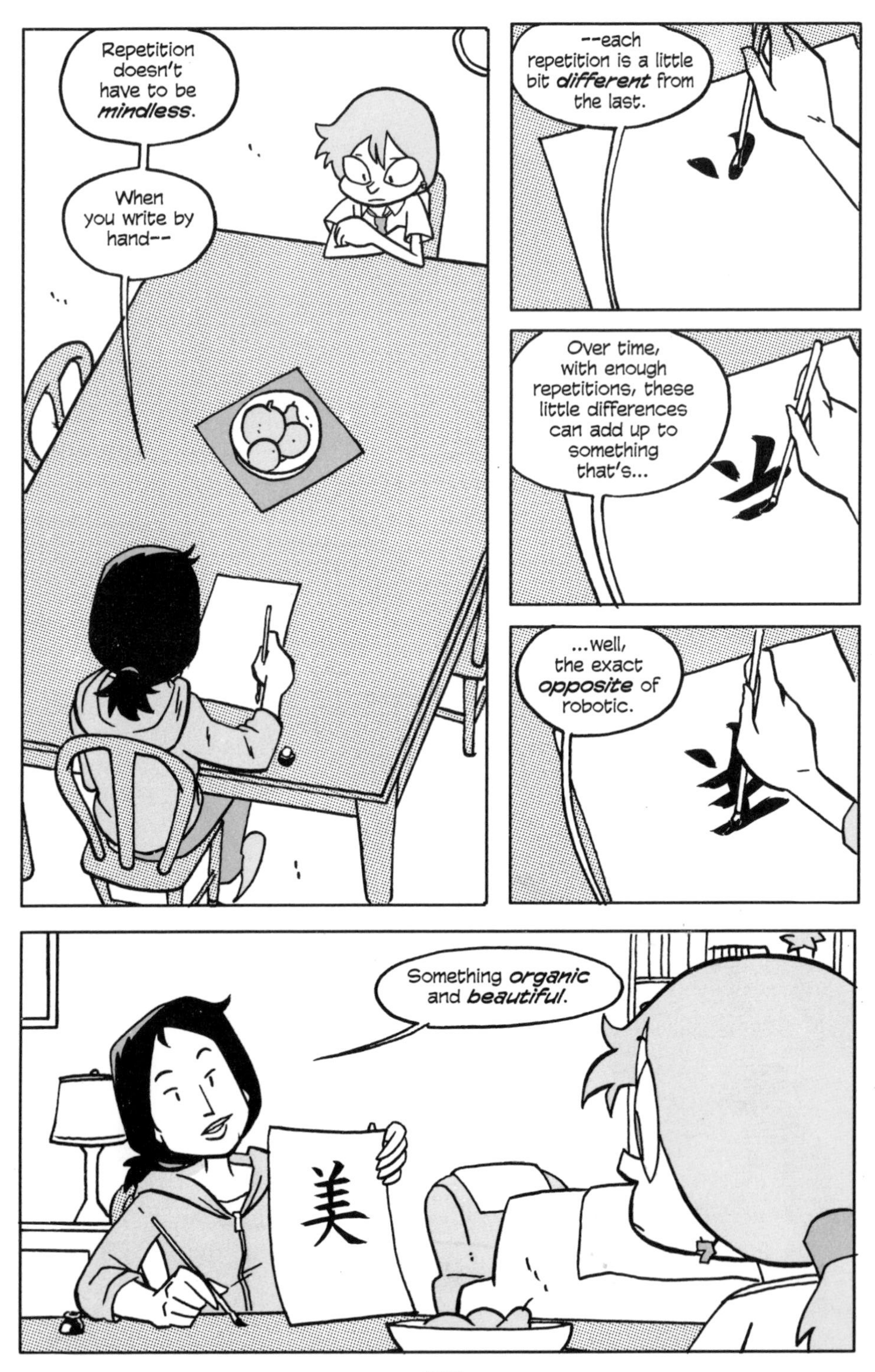
Repetition doesn't have to be *mindless*.
When you write by hand--
--each repetition is a little bit *different* from the last.
Over time, with enough repetitions, these little differences can add up to something that's...
...well, the exact *opposite* of robotic.
Something *organic* and *beautiful*.
美

So you know how to write Chinese words. Impressive, Mom. I guess you are qualified to teach Mandarin.
Where are you going? I need your help with dinner.
Sorry, I've got basketball practice tonight.
Let me give you a ride.
No thanks. I'd rather walk.

Hey! What are you guys doing here?
Came to check out your practice.
Plus, maybe we could go find Professor Bee afterwards.
...
So are we friends now?
Ow!
Now we're friends.
Meet you guys here when I'm done!

Number Seven?
Why are *you* here?
What...?
I'm sorry, young lady. There are only so many spots on the roster.
Badminton is starting up in a couple of weeks. I'm sure--
Coach, what're you saying?
You got *cut*, girl.
SPARTANS
Hopper, wait!
You didn't have to say it like *that*.
Sometimes the truth *hurts*, Eni-baby.
You gotta get through it *quick*, like pulling off a Band Aid!
You'll understand when you're older.
SPARTANS
SPARTANS

Hopper, stop.
You! Is that why you came?! Did you know that was going to happen?!
Aw, come on! Give me more credit than that!
Guys, shhh. You hear that?
Footsteps?
We're being followed!
CLOMP CLOMP CLOMP CLOMP CLOMP CLOMP CLOMP
This way, across the lawn.

Rugby players!
You know them?
I met them outside the principal's office. I don't wanna talk about it.
Come out, Dork Girl!
We know you're hiding out there somewhere!

You're Dork Girl?
I said I don't wanna talk about it!
Man, how do eighth graders get so *big?* That one guy's taller than my dad! And *hairier!*
No way we can outrun them!
Not unless we slow them down somehow.
!
Eni, you still got Little Guy with you?
Always.
I got an *idea*. You know that program we saw earlier today, the one for the *lawn-mowing turtle?*
You think we could write a program that--
That's a *great idea*, Hopper. It won't be hard at all.
What, you two got a *psychic link* or something?
Hopper and I are both *coders*. And coders think a certain way.
As soon as he said it, I knew it was true.
Yeah, that's right...we're *coders*.

Josh, we're going to dictate a program.
Can you type it in?
No problem!
We just wanna have a *chat!* Promise it won't take long!
We won't *hurt* you or your little dork friends!
Much.
Har har har!
Okay. It's done!
Looks great!
To GoodRiddanceJerkfaces
Make "Length 20
Repeat 20 [
Forward :Length
Make "Length (:Length - 1)
Right 35
]
End

?
You know the routine by now.
Before I tell you the next part, take a moment to think over the program we just created. Can you figure it out?
Can you figure out what we made the turtle do?

Chapter

The program we created was kind of like Professor Bee's lawn-mowing program, only in reverse.
Oh, Dork Girl! Come out, come out, wherever you are!
GoodRiddance Jerkfaces
To GoodRiddanceJerkfaces
Make "Length 20
Repeat 20 [
Forward :Length
Make "Length (:Length - 1)
Right 35
]
End
LENGTH
20
To GoodRiddanceJerkfaces
Make "Length 20
Repeat 20 [
Forward :Length
Make "Length (:Length - 1)
Right 35
]
End
LENGTH
20
20
Shhh! Listen! You hear that?
Dork Girl? That you?!

To GoodRiddanceJerkfaces
Make "Length 20
Repeat 20 [
Forward :Length
Make "Length (:Length - 1)
Right 35
]
End
LENGTH
20
I don't think it's her...it doesn't sound human!
Yeah... sounds like slithering!
To GoodRiddanceJerkfaces
Make "Length 20
Repeat 20 [
Forward :Length
Make "Length (:Length - 1)
Right 35
]
End
LENGTH
19
Like a snake?! Aw man, I can't deal with snakes!
There aren't any snakes on campus! And even if there were, we could take 'em!
To GoodRiddanceJerkfaces
Make "Length 20
Repeat 20 [
Forward :Length
Make "Length (:Length - 1)
Right 35
]
End
LENGTH
19
19
Captain, we gotta get outta here!
Huddle up, men! Now!

To GoodRiddanceJerkfaces
Make "Length 20
Repeat 20 [
Forward :Length
Make "Length (:Length - 1)
Right 35
]
End
LENGTH
19
Who are we?!
Stately Academy Rugby!
To GoodRiddanceJerkfaces
Make "Length 20
Repeat 20 [
Forward :Length
Make "Length (:Length - 1)
Right 35
]
End
LENGTH
18
And do we fear anything?!
Well--
Usually not--
but snakes--
To GoodRiddanceJerkfaces
Make "Length 20
Repeat 20 [
Forward :Length
Make "Length (:Length - 1)
Right 35
]
End
Men! Do we fear anything?!
No!
18
LENGTH
18

Twenty repetitions later, we had them right where we wanted them.
Hey look, Captain! You were right! It's not a snake after all!

Pull!

!
Hey, Josh--
Way ahead of you!
SPLOOOSH!
Shouldn't we take this opportunity to run?
Are you *crazy?!* We got them *trapped!*
Why were you following us?

Yeah! What do you jerk-faces want?!
Hey, *Dork Girl*, how many players are on a rugby team?
Who cares?!
You will in a second. The answer's *fifteen*.
!
Oggy! Oggy! Oggy!
Oi! Oi! Oi!
TACKLE!
TACKLE!
TACKLE!

WAP!!!
TACKLE!
This must be what *Principal Dean* was looking for!
You sure?
He said it'd be a *turtle*, didn't he?
But he said it'd be the *"most powerful turtle in the world!"* That look like the most powerful turtle in the world to you?
What it looks like is our ticket to *new uniforms!* Come on, boys! Let's get outta here!
You okay, Hopper?
I'm fine. ***Miffed***, but fine.
I-I'm all right, too. Thanks for asking.
Oggy! Oggy! Oggy!
Oi! Oi! Oi!

Hopper! Wake up!
We're leaving in *ten minutes!*
I'm up! I'm up!
I can't have you coming home so *late* on school nights!
WHUMP
I'm sorry, but if this continues, I'll have to pull you out of basketball.
Don't worry, Ma. Coach is way ahead of you.

I'm getting in the car!
Ugh.
Hopper!
Right behind you, Ma!

Hey.
Hey.
You think we should tell Professor Bee what happened--
Aw, man! You guys sore from last night?
I have to hold my arm like this for it not to feel like--
Ow!
Don't tell me you're still mad at me!
Who's mad? Maybe I just don't like you.
As I was saying before I was so rudely interrupted--we gotta tell Professor Bee about what happened to Little Guy, right? He needs to know!
Not yet.

But the guilt is killing me!
But what if he stops teaching us? I want a chance to make it right.
How're we gonna make it right?
Shhh. Here he comes.
H-Hi, Professor!
Good day, children! I must admit, I've come to look forward to these sessions with you!
Who knew trash duty could be so delightful?
Come along!

I have something *wonderful* to share with you today!
Eni, may I borrow your chalk?
Make
Take a look at this instruction. Any guesses as to what it does?
Make "Length (Random 100)
Hopper, you've been awfully quiet. What's on your mind?
Nothing! Nothing at all!
I could've told you *that*.
All right, then.
Ow!
How about you, Eni?
Make "Length (Random 100)
..
Well, this first part makes a *variable* called *Length* in the turtle's brain.
I'm not sure about this part, though. What does *Random* mean, and what's the *one hundred* for?

The Random command tells the turtle to randomly pick a number that's larger than or equal to zero, but less than one hundred.
gth (Random 100
It's as if he has a little roulette wheel in his brain. Along the edges of the wheel are the numbers zero through ninety-nine.
The instruction tells him to give the wheel a spin--
--then take the winning number--
--and put it in the variable Length.
LENGTH
36
Ah, back on your game, Hopper. Very good.
Let me write out an entire program.
Eni, please take out the robot turtle you so affectionately call "Little Guy."
WRITE WRITE

Uh...Here's the thing, Professor Bee. We--
--left him at home. We'll bring him back tomorrow. Promise.
I see. Let's use this one instead, then.
That's a turtle?
One of the first ones we ever built. We named him Irving.
Josh, would you key my program into the terminal over there?
No problem, Professor!
And please, no silly names. Let's just leave it as DrawSquare.
Aw. No fun.
tk
tk
tk
Done!
To DrawSquare
Make "Length (Random 100)
Repeat 4 [
Forward :Length
Right 90
]
End
Now, when we tell him to DrawSquare, he'll randomly select a number between zero and ninety-nine and put it in Length.
Then he'll draw a square where every side is equal to Length.

That means every time we tell him to DrawSquare, he'll draw a square of a different size.
That's right!
I wanna see it in action!
?
DrawSquare
To DrawSquare
Make "Length (Random 100)
Repeat 4 [
Forward :Length
Right 90
]
End
Whrrrrrrr!!!
To DrawSquare
Make "Length (Random 100)
Repeat 4 [
Forward :Length
Right 90
]
End
tk! tk! tk... tk
To DrawSquare
Make "Length (Random 100)
Repeat 4 [
Forward :Length
Right 90
]
End
LENGTH
72

Once.
To DrawSquare
Make "Length (Random 100)
Repeat 4 [
Forward :Length
Right 90
]
End
72
Twice.
To DrawSquare
Make "Length (Random 100)
Repeat 4 [
Forward :Length
Right 90
]
End
72
Three times.
To DrawSquare
Make "Length (Random 100)
Repeat 4 [
Forward :Length
Right 90
]
End
72
And one last time to complete the square!
To DrawSquare
Make "Length (Random 100)
Repeat 4 [
Forward :Length
Right 90
]
End
72

Go ahead. Ask Irving to do it a few more times.
?
DrawSquare
LENGTH
45
45
45
45
45
?
DrawSquare
LENGTH
89
89
89
89
89

The squares are *different sizes* every time!
That's what random *means*, dummy.
I want to try something.
?
Repeat 4 [
DrawSquare
Right 90
]
Whoa! That's so *wicked*, Eni! How'd you figure that out?
I wanna do that! Only *better!*
?
Repeat 8 [
DrawSquare
Right 45
]

Eni and I did the same thing a few more times and soon the floor was covered with all these crazy designs.
It's beautiful!
So suddenly your arm's okay?
I was healed by beauty.
Children, what you've accomplished today is quite remarkable! You took a few rudimentary concepts and combined them into something all your own!
It's because we're coders!
You don't get to call yourself that! What code did you write?!
This reminds me so much of the Bee School in its heyday!
And you, Hopper, remind me so much of your father.
So you did know him!

Many years ago, *Albert Gracie* was my student here at the Bee School. How is he now?
I...I'm *not sure*. I haven't seen him in a while. Professor, you gotta tell me--
BBRINNG
We'll have to continue this conversation later, Hopper.
Aaargh! Stupid bell! Do you always have to ring at the *worst times* ever?!
Be sure to bring Little Guy back next time. We've got plenty more learning to do with him.
We will, Professor. *Promise*.
So if this guy's called Irving, does Little Guy have a *normal name?*
Long ago, he was called Pascal Junior, after the student who helped me build him.
But I think it best that you continue to call him *Little Guy*.
Looking forward to our next session! Thank you, children, for restoring my *trust* in humanity!
Did he have to use the word *trust?!* Oh *the guilt*, the guilt!
Let's meet *tonight*, after Josh and I are done with our game. We have to figure out how to get Little Guy back.

PASS!
POP!
Go Eni!
That's my boy!
Hey, look! It's Number Seven!
Don't call me that. I'm not that anymore. My name's Hopper.
Huh. Weird name for a girl.
Weird name for anybody.
Be nice girls! Good to meet you, Hopper! I'm Mr. Wesson and this is Mrs. Wesson.
You here to cheer for Eni?
Of course you are.
Oooooo!
Girls, shhh! We're watching the game!

SWISH!!
Ha ha! He gets his jump shot from you, dear!
Oh, no! That's all you, dear!
You know, Hopper, Mrs. Wesson was something else back in her day!
Not compared to Mr. Wesson! He missed the NBA by this much!
Now now, dear. No need to bring up ancient history!
You're right, especially when the present's so exciting! You see that man in the hat?
I think he's a high school coach!
SWISH

The boys' team deserved all the attention they got. They played a great game.
Especially Eni.
Young man, I'm Coach Sanchez from **St. Sebastian's College Prep**.
Hi.
If you don't have other plans, I'd like to take you and your parents out for a *meal*.
Oh, how *wonderful!*
Go ahead, Eni. I'll tell her we can meet some other time.
Sorry, Coach. I got work to do.
What?!

Eni! I'm sure whatever you've got can wait!
No, Ma. It can't.
Now now, dear. We've always said academics come first.
No, dear. That's what you've always said!
It's all right, Mrs. Wesson.
You've got a big game coming up against your archrivals the Kennedy Cougars. I'll see you then.
And next time, I won't take no for an answer.
Homework is important, dear.
Eni, what did you just do?!
Getting into St. Sebastian's is harder than getting into Fort Knox!
I promised Professor Bee we'd bring Little Guy back, so that's what we're doing tonight.
But first, let's give Hopper her present.
You got me a present?!

Look, I know I was kind of a jerk--
Jerk-*face*.
--jerk-*face* to you, so I really appreciate you letting me hang out with you guys.
After Stan moved away, I was so *lonely*.
Stan? Who's *Stan?*
That was *Joshie's* real name.
On the first day of kindergarten, I told him he had to change his name or I wouldn't play with him.
That's *horrible!*
It was for his own *good!* Stan is a *stupid* name!
Anyway, here.
There are three of them, one for each of us.
No. Way.
GRACIE-HU

The three of us are a *team* now, right?
So we ought to have *team jerseys*.
CODERS 1000
CODERS 1010
CODERS 0111
CODERS
Guess you're not a jerk-face *all the time*.

I need to head home soon. Let's go.
Go where?
To *Principal Dean's office*. We're going to *break in* and get Little Guy back.
What?! That's your *big plan*, Eni?!
How do you even know if Little Guy's actually there?
CODERS
You heard what the *rugby players* said--
Oggy! Oggy! Oggy!
Speak of the *devil--!*
CODERS
Quick! Hide!
1000
It's *Principal Dean!* And they've got *Little Guy* with them!
See? I was right.
How come we're always hiding in bushes?!
Oi! Oi! Oi!

Gasp!
Professor Bee!
You won't get away with this, Dean!

Oh, I'm pretty sure I will, Bee!
It's in here, you say?
Yes. Now let me go!

Not yet.

Come on, Coders!
CODERS
1010

That big one there--that's the turtle you're looking for!
That's the most powerful turtle in the world?
Not quite what I was expecting.
I thought the professor said that was the lawn-mowing turtle!
Shhh.
I'm warning you, Bee! If you're lying to me, I'll have the boys break your fingers!
Uh... Principal Dean? I'm pretty sure I'd get grounded if I did that.
We gotta help the professor somehow!
We need to create a distraction.
Not just a distraction--chaos!

Let's make that lawn-mowing turtle move around *randomly!* It'll *confuse* those jerk-faces and buy us enough time to get Professor Bee out of here!
All right, ready? It's that time again.
I'm going to *stop* and you're going to *think*.
Good idea. We'll make him move forward a *random number* of units, then turn a *random angle*.
He'll repeat it over and over, maybe *a hundred* times.
CODERS
Give it a go. See if you can come up with the *program* Eni described, one that makes the turtle move randomly.
It'll help you *remember* who you are.

Continued in

Secrets & Sequences

Ready to start coding?

Visit www.secret-coders.com

Hopper Explains Angles
You know the number part of a Right or Left command?
It's called an angle.
Right 90
It tells the robot turtle how far to turn.
The bigger the angle--
45°
--the bigger the turn.
90°
An angle of 180 turns the turtle backwards.
180°
An angle of 360 turns him all the way around.
360°
If it seems a little weird, don't worry. You'll get it.
I mean, even Josh got it.
Hey!